FIREMAN SAM
AND THE BONFIRE

story by Diane Wilmer
illustrations by The County Studio

GUILD PUBLISHING
LONDON · NEW YORK · SYDNEY · TORONTO

Sarah and James were playing football in Fireman
Sam's back garden.

"Watch out for my windows," laughed Fireman Sam.

"And for my washing," called Trevor Evans. "I've
just washed my best shirt."

"We'll be careful," promised Sarah.

"It's my birthday today and Bella's invited me round for supper," said Trevor. "So I've got to look extra-specially smart tonight."

"We won't dirty your clean shirt," promised James.

Sarah kicked the ball to James. WHACK! It bounced
past him and landed on top of Fireman Sam's
rubbish heap.

"Bother!" said Sarah. "Now what do we do?"

"We'll have to get it down," said James.

"How?" asked Sarah.

James looked around. "Maybe I can get it down
with the rake," he said.

He poked the top of the heap with the long rake and the ball came tumbling down. So did Fireman Sam's rubbish heap.

"We'd better tidy it up a bit," said Sarah.

"All right," agreed James.

They started to pile up the fallen wood.

Suddenly, something flashed past James.

"Oh! What was that?" he cried.

"I don't know," said Sarah. "I think it ran under the rubbish heap."

They peeped inside the tangled heap. It was musty and dark.

"I can't see anything," said Sarah.

"Wait," hissed James. "Look, there! Something's moving."

Sarah stared hard. "It's a little mouse!" she cried.

"Ssshhhsh!" whispered James. "Let's see where it goes."

The mouse scurried into a bundle of leaves and dried grass. Lots of tiny mice started to wriggle around her.

"She's got babies!" squeaked Sarah.

"Come away," said James. "We don't want to frighten them."

"All right," said Sarah. "Let's tidy the heap and then leave them alone."

They picked up their ball and crept to the end of the garden.

"Shall we tell Uncle Sam?" said James.

"No," said Sarah. "Let's keep it a secret."

They went indoors to have some lemonade with Fireman Sam.

A moment later, Trevor Evans came out to take his washing off the line. "Mmmm, my shirt's still a bit damp," he said. "I'll leave it out while I pop to the shops, then I'll iron it when I get back."

Sarah and James finished their drink then offered to go shopping for Fireman Sam.

"I'll have a loaf of brown bread and a jar of peanut butter, please, and there'll be enough change left for two ice-creams," he smiled.

"Thanks, Uncle Sam!" cried James and Sarah, and they ran off down the road.

Fireman Sam finished weeding his flower bed then swept the garden path and put all the rubbish in his wheelbarrow. He pushed it round to the back garden and piled all the rubbish onto the heap.

"Goodness, I'll have to do something about this lot," gasped Fireman Sam. "Maybe I'll light a bonfire to get rid of it."

He looked over the fence to see whether Trevor had taken in his washing. The line looked empty.

"I think I'll light the fire now, while Trevor's out," thought Fireman Sam. "Then he won't be bothered by the smoke."

He didn't notice the shirt still on the line in a corner of the garden. And he didn't know anything about the family of mice living in the rubbish heap.

Down in Pontypandy, Trevor was chatting to Bella inside her cafe, while the twins were eating their ice-creams outside Dilys's shop and chatting to Norman, Dilys's son.

"Look up there," yelled Norman, suddenly. "Fireman Sam's garden is on fire!"

"Don't be silly, Norman," sniffed Dilys. "It's just a little bonfire. Fireman Sam is probably tidying up his garden."

Sarah dropped her ice-cream.

"A bonfire!" she cried. "Oh no!"

"We've got to stop him!" yelled James.

When Trevor heard all the shouting he ran across the road.

"What's going on?" he asked.

"Uncle Sam's lit a bonfire in his garden," said Sarah.

"And there's a mouse in it, with lots of little babies," said James.

"Oh no!" yelled Trevor. "And what about my best shirt?"

They ran up the hill to the fire station and Sarah rang the fire bell. RING-A-LING-LING!

Fireman Elvis Cridlington came running to the door, wiping tomato ketchup off his face.

"Hey! What's up?" he asked.

"There's a fire in Fireman Sam's garden," said Trevor.

"And we've got to put it out," cried James.

"It's an emergency!" yelled Sarah.

Elvis jumped into Jupiter's driving seat and
switched on the siren.

"Right Fireman Cridlington," said Fire Officer
Steele. "Off we go."

Fireman Sam looked up when he heard Jupiter's
siren wailing.

"Goodness me! I wonder what's on fire?" he worried.

He couldn't believe his eyes when Jupiter stopped right outside his own house!

"Elvis!" called Fireman Sam. "What's wrong?"

"FIRE!" cried Elvis.

"We've got to put out your bonfire, Fireman Sam," said Fire Officer Steele.

"Quick! Quick!" shouted James and Sarah as they rushed up the hill.

Elvis came running up the path with the fire hose
and Fire Officer Steele turned on the water.

"Stop! What *is* going on?" shouted Fireman Sam.

"Sorry Sir," gasped Elvis. "I'll explain later. This is
a real emergency!"

The water came spurting through the nozzle and
Elvis aimed it at the bonfire. WHOOOOSH! In
seconds the fire was out.

"That's done it," said Elvis.

"It certainly has," snapped Fireman Sam. "Now, will somebody please tell me what you're doing with that hose?"

"There's a mouse living in the bonfire, Uncle Sam," said Sarah.

"She had a nest under there," said James. "With lots of babies in it."

"Oh dear," said Fireman Sam. "Why didn't you tell me?"
"We wanted to keep it a secret," said Sarah.
Trevor came marching up.
"I'm furious, Fireman Sam!" he roared. "You're
supposed to be a good neighbour. Didn't you see my
shirt hanging on the washing line."

"Of course I didn't," cried Fireman Sam. "I looked over the fence and I couldn't see it!"

"I left it in the corner," moaned Trevor.

"No wonder I couldn't see it," said Fireman Sam.

"Hmmm!" sniffed Trevor. "Now I'll have to wash it all over again!"

Trevor stomped off to look at his shirt. Fireman Sam
and the twins poked around underneath the dripping
bonfire. There was no sign of the mouse or her babies.
  "Where can she be?" asked Sarah.
  "I don't know," said Fireman Sam. "But I *do* know I
wish I'd never lit that bonfire."
  "So do I," muttered Trevor, from over the fence. "Just
look at my best shirt. Now what will I wear to Bella's
tonight?" snapped Trevor and crossly kicked at the
leaves around his rhubarb plant.
  "SQUEAK! SQUEAK! SQUEAK! SQUEAK!"
  "It's the mice!" cried James. "They must have escaped
into Trevor's garden when Uncle Sam lit the bonfire."

They hurried round to Trevor's garden and rushed up the path.

"Quiet now," warned Trevor. "We don't want to frighten them again."

Fireman Sam bent down and very gently lifted up the big green rhubarb leaves. Tucked underneath them was an old watering can, full of leaves and snuggled inside it was the mouse with all her babies.

"They're safe," whispered Sarah.

"Safe as houses," said Fireman Sam.

"Well I never," laughed Trevor. "I've been wondering where that old watering can was!"

"Come on, let's leave them alone," said Fireman Sam. "I think they've had enough excitement for one day."

"I must take Jupiter back to the Fire Station," said
Elvis, rolling up the hose.
　"Hold on a minute, we'll come with you," called
Fireman Sam. "I want to pop into Bella's."
　"You can tell her I'll be late," said Trevor.
　They left him behind, washing his shirt for the
second time that day.

Elvis dropped them off outside Bella's cafe and the three of them walked in. They found Bella icing Trevor's birthday cake.

"His favourite cake," said Bella. "Chocolate cream, with fudge filling. He will love it, I know."

"I'm sure he will," said Fireman Sam, nervously. "But he'll be a bit late. Er ... you see Bella, there's been a bit of an accident."

"Accident!" cried Bella. "What happened? Is Trevor all right?"

"Yes," said Sarah. "But his best shirt isn't."

"He washed it," explained James. "So he'd look extra-specially smart for you tonight."

"But I didn't see it hanging on the line," said Fireman Sam. "And I lit a bonfire and blew smoke all over it."

"He's washing his shirt again, and he asked us to tell you he'll be late," said James.

Bella burst out laughing. "Oh! You mustn't worry!" she chuckled. "Just look what I've bought him for his birthday."

She held up a shiny packet and they all stared at it. "A new shirt!" cried Fireman Sam.

"A beautiful shirt!" laughed Bella. "Here, James and Sarah, take this to Trevor and tell him to come quickly. His birthday supper is ready and waiting!"

FIREMAN SAM SAYS:

bonfires can be a nuisance. Before a
grown-up lights one, they should make sure
it won't annoy the neighbours.

This edition published 1989 by Guild Publishing
by arrangement with William Heinemann Ltd

First published 1988 by William Heinemann
Fireman Sam © 1985 Prism Art & Design Ltd
Text © 1988 William Heinemann Ltd
Illustrations © 1988 William Heinemann Ltd
All rights reserved

Based on the animation series produced by Bumper Films
for S4C – Channel 4 Wales – and Prism Art & Design Ltd

Original idea by Dave Gingell and Dave Jones, assisted
by Mike Young

Characters created by Rob Lee

Printed in Great Britain by
Springbourne Press Ltd